Cuddle

The Magic Kitten

SCHOOL OF SPELLS

Cuddle
The Magic Kitten

SCHOOL OF SPELLS

by Hayley Daze

A CIP catalogue record for this book is
available from the British Library

This edition published by Willow Tree Books, 2019
Willow Tree Books, Tide Mill Way, Woodbridge, Suffolk, IP12 1AP
First published by Ladybird Books Ltd.

0 2 4 6 8 9 7 5 3 1

Series created by Working Partners Limited,
London, WC1X 9HH

Special thanks to Elizabeth Galloway

ISBN: 978-1-78958-038-9
Printed and bound in Great Britain
by Bell and Bain Ltd, Glasgow

www.willowtreebooks.net

For Emily and Jessica Cowlard and
Lottie Perryman - wishing you all
many magical adventures

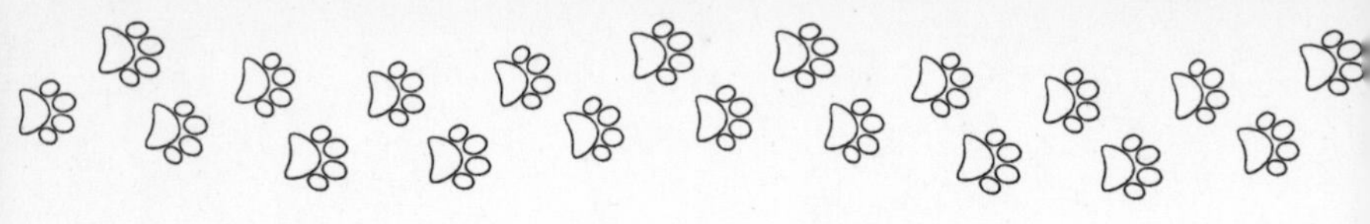

Cuddle the kitten has black-and-white fur,
A cute crooked tail, and a very loud purr.
Her two best friends, Olivia and Grace,
Know Cuddle's world is a special place!

Just give her a cuddle, then everything spins;
A twitch of her whiskers, and magic begins!
So if you see a sunbeam, and hear Cuddle's bell,
You can join in the adventures as well!

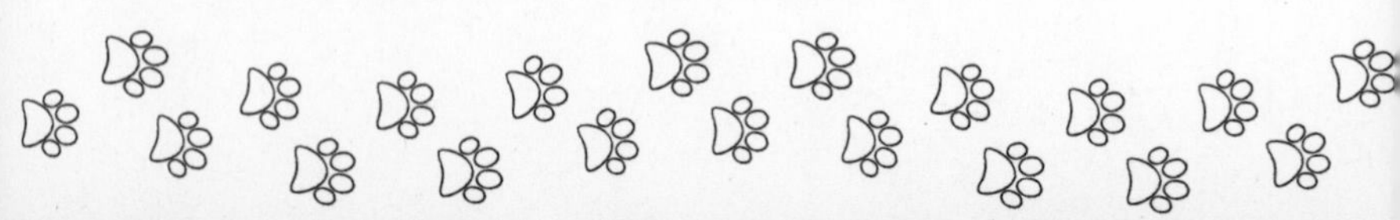

Contents

Chapter One
Fairy Fun

Olivia squeezed her eyes shut. "Abracadabra, fiddle-dee-dee, show me my wand, as fast as can be!"

She opened her eyes again and looked at the dressing-up box on the lawn of her back garden. A pirate hat, face paints and a pink feather boa were

spilling out of it, but Olivia sighed.

"I can't see my wand anywhere," she said to Grace.

The two girls were in fancy dress. Olivia's fairy outfit was a purple leotard and tutu, and pink net wings covered in silver sparkle. Her mum had made the outfit for Olivia on her sewing machine. Slung over her shoulder was the little bag she took everywhere. Grace was dressed up as an elf, in a green T-shirt and shorts, and plastic pointy ears hooked over her real ones.

"Don't worry," Grace said. "My mum says I'm good at finding things. When we lived on a farm, I used to look for where the chickens had laid their eggs.

I'll help you find your wand."

It was a grey day in Catterton, with clouds hanging low over the houses and blocks of flats. Olivia and Grace had decided to brighten up the garden, turning it into a fairy grotto. Olivia had strung daisy chains from the branches of the trees, while Grace had lined up her mum's garden gnome collection on top of the fence.

The girls knelt beside the pot plants on the patio, searching for the wand among the leaves and flowers.

"If only I was a proper fairy," Olivia said, "then I could use magic to find it."

Grace jumped up, her eyes shining. "We do know someone with real magic."

"Cuddle!" cried Olivia.

The girls grinned at each other. Cuddle was a magical kitten who took them on amazing adventures.

Suddenly, a beam of sunlight reached through the clouds. It shimmered in the air like a golden rainbow, shining right on to the dressing-up box.

Jingle jangle jingle.

"That's Cuddle's bell!" Grace cried. "She's here!"

The girls ran towards the dressing-up box and looked inside. Its contents wobbled and quivered, and a black tail with a kink in its tip poked through. Then came a pair of black paws, and finally a furry white face.

"Cuddle!" Olivia said. "And look what she's found."

The kitten had a plastic purple wand in her mouth. Olivia took it gently and tucked it inside her bag.

"Clever Cuddle," Grace said, and tickled the kitten under the chin, just where her purr was rumbling.

With a mew Cuddle sprang into Grace's arms, the silver bell on her pink collar jangling. Both girls shut their eyes as the kitten's purr made their skin tingle all over.

"I feel like I'm covered in fizzy sherbet," Olivia murmured. "I wonder where Cuddle will take us this time ..."

***

Grace rubbed her eyes. They were standing on a large stretch of grass. White stripes marked out a pitch, and on the edge of the playing field was a school building with iron gates and lots of little windows winking in the sunlight. Grace could hear shouts of laughter coming from a playground to the side of the building.

"Why would Cuddle bring us to a school?" she said to Olivia. "We go to school all the time."

The kitten jumped down from Olivia's arms, and scampered across the grass towards the cries of other children. But as the girls stepped into the playground, they gasped with amazement.

"Whoa!" Grace cried, gazing around her. The two of them turned in a slow circle, their eyes wide as they took everything in.

"Wheeeee!" shouted a pixie, kicking with his curly-toed shoes as he whizzed down a slide. He jumped off the slide, and Olivia could see that he only came up to her waist.

A group of elves dressed in

green were playing football against a team of gnomes dressed in red. "Goal!" yelled one of the elves. "Good shot!" shouted a gnome.

"I don't believe it," Olivia whispered. "Look!" She pointed into the air and Cuddle mewed with excitement.

Three fairies flew over their heads, pausing to flutter around a sign above a door. As they passed over, glitter fell down on to the girls. Olivia shook the glitter from her hair and laughed.

Gazing back up at the sign, she saw golden letters painted on it.

"Miss Rosamund's School for Magical Creatures," she read out loud. Olivia turned to Grace, her eyes bright.

"We're at a school for magic!"

Chapter Two
The Shy Unicorn

"Come on," Grace said. "Let's ask if we can play too!"

They ran to join the magical creatures, Cuddle skipping beside them. Grace gazed up at the fairies playing in the air above their heads.

"Your wings look just like theirs,"

she said to Olivia, pointing at the fairies.

"Hello!" one of the fairies called down. "Have you come to join Miss Rosamund's school?"

"We hope so!" Grace called back.

Cuddle scampered away, bounding towards a broad tree on the edge of the playing field. It was covered in pink, yellow and blue flowers. A white pony stood underneath it. Sticking out from his forehead was a long horn, twisted into a spiral like a seashell. It had a kink in its tip, just like Cuddle's tail.

Grace's mouth dropped open. "Look – a unicorn!"

At the sound of her voice, the

unicorn's cheeks went rosy pink. He dropped the flowers he was eating and ducked behind the tree, out of sight.

"I think he's shy," Olivia whispered.

Cuddle peered around the tree trunk, lifting her pink nose into the air.

"What's Cuddle doing?" Grace wondered.

The unicorn poked his long white muzzle out from behind the tree. He leaned down and gently touched his nose to Cuddle's. Cuddle mewed and jumped on to the unicorn's back, curling up behind his head.

"Cuddle's making friends," Olivia said, clapping her hands.

Cuddle's tail brushed against the

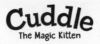

unicorn's cheek. "Neigh-heehee!" he snorted, shaking as if Cuddle was tickling him. The unicorn skipped around the tree trunk, picking his hooves up high. Cuddle gave a happy mew as she bounced on his back.

"Wow," Grace said. "He's a brilliant dancer!"

The unicorn stopped dancing and his eyelashes fluttered. "Thank you," he said.

"You can talk!" Olivia gasped. "Please don't be scared of us. I'm Olivia. This is Grace, and you've met Cuddle, our kitten."

"I'm Cosmo," the unicorn said, quietly.

"Nice to meet you, Cosmo," Grace said. "Why don't we go and play with the others?"

"Because no one wants to play with a silly unicorn," a voice said.

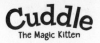

The girls looked round. Standing beside them was a troll. His skin was green and warty, and he had yellow eyes. The troll jammed his thumbs into his ears and waggled his fingers, sticking out his tongue.

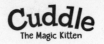

"Stupid putrid Cosmo!" he jeered.

Olivia put her hands on her hips. "Stop it! Calling people names is nasty."

The troll stuck his tongue out again and walked off.

Grace patted Cosmo's silky mane. "Let's go and play," she said.

But Cosmo hung his head and sighed.

Olivia took Grace's hand, pulling her aside. "I think he's too shy to join in," she whispered. "And that troll's making him feel even worse."

"That must be why Cuddle's brought us here," Grace said. "To help Cosmo make friends!"

Chapter Three

Miss Rosamund Arrives

Tinkle tinkle tinkle.

"What's that?" Grace asked.

"It's Miss Rosamund," Cosmo said. "She's our head teacher."

Tinkle tinkle tinkle.

Puff! A lady with silver hair appeared in an explosion of glitter.

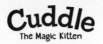

She was wearing a pink gown, and in one hand she had a silver wand with a star on top. In the other, she held a silver bell. Miss Rosamund tinkled the bell. "Time for lessons!" she called, her cheeks dimpling as she smiled. "Come on, everyone! You're all going to learn

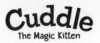

your own special magic today."

Olivia gasped. "Well, that beats learning times tables!"

Miss Rosamund walked into the school building, the magical creatures skipping along behind her. Cuddle flicked her crooked tail and ran through the open doorway to join them.

"Good idea, Cuddle," Grace said. "We can learn about magic too. Come on, Cosmo!"

They hurried after the little kitten. But the troll crawled out from under the slide.

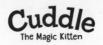

"Looking forward to the magic lessons?" he asked Cosmo.

"Yes," Cosmo replied, backing away.

"Why?" the troll demanded. "Silly unicorns can't do magic. Everyone's going to laugh at you!"

"Hey," Grace said. "We've already told you to stop being mean."

"Parp!" The troll made a loud raspberry sound and bounded after the other creatures.

"Just ignore him, Cosmo," Olivia said.

But the unicorn was already trotting back towards the tree, his head drooping. Grace scooped up Cuddle and the girls ran to join him.

"Please come to the lesson," Grace said. "You might make some new friends."

Tears glittered like jewels on Cosmo's long eyelashes. "But I can't do magic. Why would anyone want to be friends with a unicorn who isn't magical?"

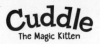

Chapter Four
Whizzing Wands

"Miaow!" Cuddle wiggled her whiskers. The branches above them rustled, and hundreds of pink, yellow and blue petals showered down. They caught in Cosmo's mane and Olivia's fairy wings, and stuck on to Grace's pointy ears. Cuddle flicked a petal off her nose with

her pink tongue.

Cosmo's eyes were wide. "Did Cuddle make this happen?" he asked.

Grace nodded. "She's a magical kitten. If a little kitten like Cuddle can make magic, I'm sure a unicorn can too! She wants to help you, Cosmo – and so do we. Please go to the magic lesson!"

"Alright," he agreed. "But only if you and Olivia come too."

Grace threw her arms around Cosmo's long neck. "Of course we will!"

Olivia glanced towards the school door, where the other pupils had gone in with Miss Rosamund. "And we'd

better hurry," she added, "or we'll be late for the lesson."

Cosmo knelt down on the lawn, folding his legs beneath him. "All aboard the Cosmo Express!" he said.

Grace gently held on to Cosmo's mane and pulled herself on to his back. She'd ridden lots of ponies before, but never a unicorn! Olivia sat behind, her arms around Grace's waist. Cuddle sprang into Grace's lap.

Cosmo stood up and galloped towards the school building. He skipped from hoof to hoof, his tail swishing along to the rhythm of his steps.

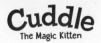

"Woohoo!" Grace cheered. "This is an amazing galloping dance, Cosmo!"

As they approached the school door, Cosmo ducked his head beneath the frame and trotted down the corridor, his hooves clip-clopping. The girls gasped as each floor tile lit up red, yellow or blue as Cosmo stepped over them.

"It's magic!" Grace cried.

Cosmo gave a gentle neigh. "Of course it is. We're in a magic school, remember?"

Soon they arrived outside a classroom and the girls slid from Cosmo's back. Then they followed him inside. Grace sank on to a plump cushion beside the elves, gnomes and fairies who were arranged in a circle around Miss Rosamund. Olivia sat down beside her on a purple velvet cushion. On the shelves around the classroom were little cauldrons, glass

jars stuffed full of magic wands and piles of glitter dust.

"I've never been in a classroom like this before," Grace whispered to Olivia.

"Hello, Cosmo," Miss Rosamund said. "I see you've brought two new pupils."

Cosmo knelt down beside the girls. Cuddle leapt down from his back, landing at Miss Rosamund's feet.

"And who have we here?" she asked.

"That's Cuddle," Olivia explained. "I'm Olivia and this is Grace."

"Welcome to you all," Miss Rosamund said. "I usually ring my bell to show that the lesson has started, but maybe Cuddle could ring hers today."

The little kitten shook her head, making her bell jingle. The magical creatures giggled, and Cuddle hopped on to Olivia's knee.

Miss Rosamund waved her silver wand, and to the girls' amazement, wooden bookcases appeared out of thin air. Even though they were crammed with books, they hovered above the floor.

Olivia's eyes darted over their spines. "Flying for Beginners, 101

Tricks to Play on Humans, Magic Made Easy," she read in a whisper. "They're all about magic."

Miss Rosamund walked over to a large desk at one end of the classroom. On it was a pen pot filled with strange-looking sticks. Miss Rosamund stood behind the desk and used her wand to write pink letters in the air: "My Magical Gift".

"Wow," Grace murmured. "It's like a magical whiteboard."

"Now, class," Miss Rosamund said. "Everyone has their own special kind of magic, and today you're going to find yours."

"But how will we know when we've

found it?" a pixie asked, scratching his head.

Miss Rosamund smiled. "You'll

know," she said. "Your tummy will tingle, and you'll feel so happy you could float up into the clouds. I found my special magic when I was trying to cast a spell to make lemonade. Instead, I magicked a special teacher's cloak." She stroked the pink silk of her cloak, smiling. "That's how I knew I was meant to set up a school for magic!"

She waved her wand once more and the sticks floated out of the pen pot. They were a rainbow of colours, each with a different shape at the top.

"Magic wands!" Olivia said, bouncing up and down.

Miss Rosamund raised her hands. "Magic wands, hear my call, find your owner, one and all!"

With a whoosh, the wands whizzed over everyone's heads, like a firework display. Cuddle leapt on to Olivia's shoulder, and as a red wand with a heart at its tip zoomed past, she sprang up and caught it between her teeth. She jumped to the ground to give it to

Cosmo.

"Look, everyone else is getting their own wand too," Grace said.

A gnome cheered as he caught a green wand with a flower at the top, while a wand with a diamond shape landed on a giggling pixie's desk. Olivia opened her bag and took out her plastic wand. "You never know," she said to Grace, "we might need one too."

Miss Rosamund clapped her hands and the class turned to look at her. "Here comes the fun part," she said, her eyes twinkling. "First, I want you to split up into groups. Then each group must work together to practise your very own magic spell. Off you go!"

The creatures jumped off their cushions and rushed to join up. The gnomes immediately stood together, and so did the pixies. The elves gathered by one of the bookcases. Cosmo's cheeks reddened and he lowered his gaze to the floor.

"Oh no," Grace whispered. "The other pupils aren't mixing up at all."

"And Cosmo's the only unicorn," Olivia said. "He's going to be left out!"

Chapter Five
Mean Mossfly

Olivia ran over to three fairies who were fluttering beside Miss Rosamund's desk. "Would you like to be in a group with me and my friends?" she asked.

The fairies glanced at each other and gave a small nod. "OK, we'll be in your group!" one of them said.

Olivia led the fairies over to Cosmo. Grace was hurrying back, too, leading an elf by the hand.

"This is Hal," Grace said. "His ears are even pointier than mine."

"We're Dilly, Milly and Tilly," one of the fairies said.

"Miaow!" Cuddle trotted up to them. She was followed by a gnome with a long white beard, a red hat, and a fishing rod tucked into his belt.

"And I'm Norris," the gnome said.

The girls introduced themselves, then Grace gently nudged Cosmo forwards. "Go on," she whispered into his ear.

"I'm Cosmo," he said, very quietly.

"Well done," Olivia whispered. Aloud, she said, "Our group's ready to start, now."

"Not quite," a sneering voice said. It was the troll.

The fairy called Dilly folded her arms. "What do you want, Mossy?"

"My name's Mossfly," the troll said crossly. "I'm going to be in your group, too. I can't wait to see the useless unicorn mess this – eek!"

Cuddle had pounced on Mossfly's foot. The troll waved his leg about, trying to shake her away.

"Get off me!" he shouted.

Grace carefully peeled Cuddle off the troll. "No wonder our kitten doesn't like you," she said. "You're being mean. You can be in our group, but only if you're nice to everyone."

Mossfly scowled, but eventually he nodded in agreement.

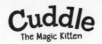

“Who wants to go first?” Olivia asked, sitting on one of the cushions. Cuddle curled up beside her.

“Me!” Hal the elf cried, taking an acorn out of his pocket. “I found this near a tree,” he explained.

He held out his wand, which had a leaf shape on the end, screwed his eyes shut, and chanted. “Huffle, puffle, float to the moon, make this acorn a blue balloon!”

With a puff, the acorn transformed into a shiny

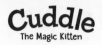

blue balloon with a long ribbon knotted to it. Hal beamed as he held it.

Grace whistled in approval, while Olivia clapped.

"You've found your gift!" Miss Rosamund cried, walking over. "Well done, Hal. You're clearly meant to work with nature."

"I'll go next," Norris the gnome said. He rubbed his tummy with one hand and waved his wand with the other. The sweetie shape at the end flashed in the sunshine. Norris said,

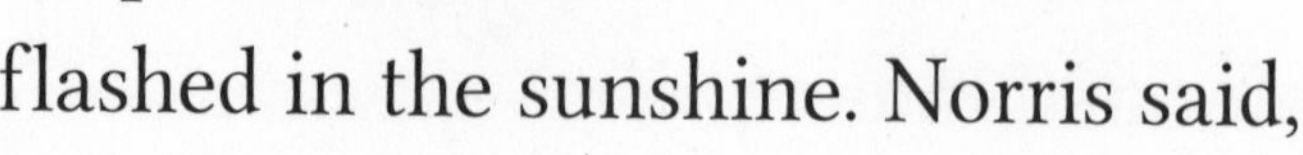

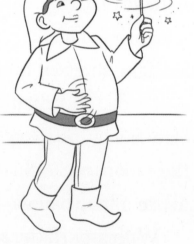

"Hizzle, fizzle, nice ice cream, make the biggest bowl I've seen!"

But no ice cream appeared. Instead, Norris's red hat turned green. Mossfly put his warty hands over his mouth as if he were trying not to laugh.

Miss Rosamund bent down. "I think your magic gift is colours, not food," she whispered in Norris's ear.

"Norris has given us an idea," Milly said. The three fairies held their wands together so the moon shapes at the end were touching. Together, they chanted, "Sugar, icing, chocolate flakes, conjure a plate of delicious cakes!"

Golden sparks fizzed from their wands and a plate of cakes appeared,

floating in the air. They were in paper cases and coated with pink icing.

"Fairy cakes!" Grace said. "Yummy! So food is your magic gift!"

"Who wants icky pink?" Mossfly said. He pointed his spider-tipped wand at the plate, and yelled, "Mud and worms, slugs and grime, cover those

nasty cakes in slime!"

With a flash, oozing green slime appeared on the cakes, dripping off them like pondweed.

"Oh no!" the fairies cried.

"Miaow!" Cuddle ran over to rub against Mossfly's ankles, her whiskers twitching.

"Stop!" Mossfly screeched. "It tickles!"

Cuddle's whiskers gave a final twitch and the slime disappeared in a cloud of green smoke.

The fairies clapped. "Thank you, Cuddle!" they said in their tinkling voices.

"It's your turn now," Olivia said to

Cosmo.

The unicorn stared at the group. His eyes were wide and his knees trembled.

"Silly scaredy Cosmo," Mossfly said. "I told you he was useless."

Cosmo shook his head from side to side, waving his wand.

"That's it!" Grace said.

But the wand slipped out from between the unicorn's teeth and plopped on to one of the cushions. "It's no good," Cosmo said. "I don't have a magical gift." Then he turned round and raced out of the classroom.

"Cosmo, come back!" Grace and Olivia cried. Had Cosmo given up on magic school for good?

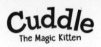

Chapter Six

Try, Try, Try Again

Cuddle followed Cosmo out into the corridor. All Grace and Olivia could hear were soft mews from Cuddle and Cosmo's neighs.

"It's almost as though they're talking to each other," Olivia said.

Grace shrugged. "Perhaps they are."

Then a cloud of silver glitter billowed into the classroom, followed by Cosmo with Cuddle riding on his back.

Olivia patted Cosmo's long neck. "I'm so glad you're back. Remember what Miss Rosamund said – we've all got a magical gift. Please try!"

"Please, Cosmo!" the three fairies begged.

"Have a go!" Hal said, waving his balloon.

"Cuddle made me think again," said Cosmo. "She says she had to work hard at her magic to begin with." The little kitten gave a mew of protest and Cosmo giggled. "Sorry, Cuddle. You didn't tell me it was a secret."

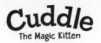

Cosmo lowered his head to pick up the wand, and Cuddle leapt back down to the floor. She touched the tip of her crooked tail to the kink in Cosmo's horn. One of her blue eyes narrowed in a wink.

"Oh," Cosmo said, nodding at the little kitten. "Cuddle's just given me an idea. I can't pick up my wand properly. I'm going to try using my horn as a wand instead."

Cosmo waved his white horn, as if he were making a spell, but nothing happened. "I still can't do it," he murmured.

Cuddle rubbed against Cosmo's front legs. Then she hopped from paw to paw, her ears flicking and her tail swishing.

"She's dancing," Grace murmured to Olivia. "Hey! If we can get Cosmo to dance, maybe he'll stop being so nervous and his spell will work."

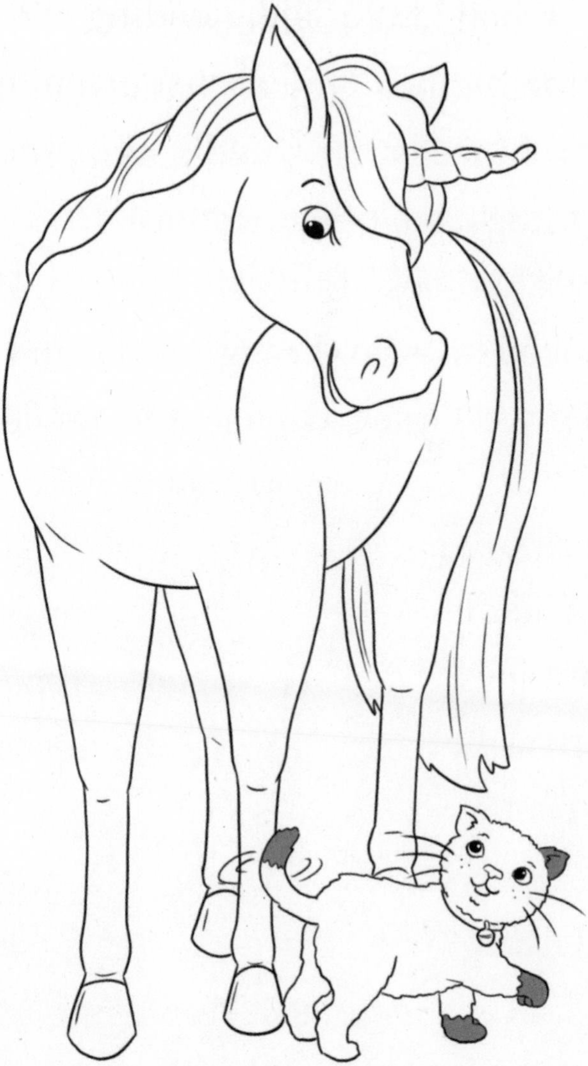

"Good idea," Olivia agreed.

Olivia took Grace's hand, and the girls danced after Cuddle, skipping and twirling each other around.

"That looks fun!" Norris said. He hooked his arm through Hal's and they followed Grace, Olivia and Cuddle.

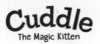

The three fairies fluttered after them, dancing on the tips of their toes like ballerinas. Even Mossfly joined in, jumping and waving his arms above his head. Cuddle led them around the cushions and in between the floating bookcases.

“Come on, Cosmo!” Olivia called. “You’re the best dancer of all!”

The unicorn’s white brow furrowed, but then he galloped after the line of dancers. His four legs were a blur as he hopped and twirled.

Grace gasped. “Look at Cosmo’s horn!” she said to Olivia.

It had burst into a rainbow of colours. As he danced, Cosmo waved his horn and chanted, “I love to eat flowers and watch clouds in the skies, but in laughter and friendship true happiness lies!”

All the dancers stopped still. Grace squeezed Olivia’s hand. Would Cosmo’s spell work?

Chapter Seven
The Gift of Friendship

"Hee hee hee," giggled Tilly the fairy.

"Ha ha ha!" chuckled Hal the elf.

"HO HO HO!" Norris the gnome bellowed.

Grace glanced at Olivia. "Are they laughing at Cosmo?" she whispered.

But Olivia's shoulders trembled.

She was giggling too! She pointed to Cosmo. The unicorn's ears quivered as he tossed his head back, giving a great snort of laughter.

"Cosmo's spell worked," Olivia said, in between chuckles.

Mossfly was still scowling. But his shoulders started to shake and his belly jiggled. "Ha! Hee!" he chortled. He threw himself on to the ground, thumping the grass with his fist. "A-hoo-hoo!"

Grace giggled. "The spell's even worked on Mossfly!"

All the other groups of creatures and Miss Rosamund hurried over.

"What's going on?" asked a pixie.

"Did someone make a joke?"

Miss Rosamund's eyes twinkled. "Perhaps Cosmo can explain."

The unicorn's crooked horn shimmered with colour. He coughed, clearing his throat, then spoke in the loudest voice the girls had heard him use. "My tummy tingles and I think I could float up into the sky," he said. "I must have f-f-found my magical gift, Miss Rosamund. It's making people laugh."

"That's wonderful news!" Miss Rosamund cried.

She hurried over to her desk, where "My Magical Gift" still hung in pink letters in the air. Holding her wand up once more, she wrote underneath:

Cosmo's Spell:
Gold Star

Then Miss Rosamund waved her wand and a golden star appeared beside her writing.

Cosmo's blue eyes widened. "I've never had a gold star before!"

"I think Cuddle deserves a star as well," Miss Rosamund said with a smile.

"Miaow!" Cuddle hopped across to Miss Rosamund and jumped into her arms. She held the little kitten in the crook of her arm, stroking the white fur on Cuddle's tummy.

"You really are the cutest kitten," Miss Rosamund said. She waved her wand, and a tiny silver star appeared on Cuddle's collar, dangling next to her bell. "There's a star for you, too, for all

your help today."

Mossfly stepped in front of the girls and the unicorn. "Er, Cosmo," the troll began. He was tapping the spidery tip of his wand against his palm, as if he were nervous. "I'm sorry I called you those names," he said. "I'm going to try to be nicer from now on."

"That's alright, Mossfly," Cosmo replied.

"Here, take this." Olivia handed the troll her plastic purple wand. "I think it suits you better than that horrible spider wand."

Mossfly gave a lopsided grin. He sat on one of the cushions, waving his new wand.

"It's not like we need wands anyway," Olivia said with a sigh. "We can't do magic."

"Oh yes, you can," Miss Rosamund said, stepping beside them. Cuddle was still in her arms, pink sparkles shimmering around both of them.

She nodded towards Cosmo. "Just look at him."

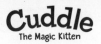

The unicorn was surrounded by the other magical creatures, his horn shining with colour.

"What do you call a unicorn that

hasn't got a horn?" Cosmo asked Hal the elf. "A u-no-horn!"

Hal doubled up with laughter, almost letting go of his balloon.

Miss Rosamund smiled at the girls. "Before Cosmo met you and Cuddle, he was shy and lonely. You've made him happy," she said. "You two have the greatest magical gift of all – the gift of friendship."

Chapter Eight
The Most Magical Gift of All

"Miaow!" Cuddle scrambled out of Miss Rosamund's arms. She nuzzled against Olivia's ankles, her fur tickling her bare skin, then wound around Grace's legs.

"It's time for Cuddle to take us home," Grace said to Miss Rosamund.

Cosmo trotted over to them, one of

the fairies perched on his back. "Before you go, I'd like to do one last magic trick."

"What's that?" Olivia asked. Cosmo swirled his horn in the air.

"Hold hands around me," he said. Grace, Olivia, Norris, Hal and the fairies all held hands, the fairies dipping and hovering in the air.

"Now start dancing," he said. As he stood in the centre of the circle, Grace and Olivia skipped around and around with all the others. Cosmo waved his horn and it burst into colour.

"Little girls and kitten too, here's a gift from us to you." He gave a final swirl of his horn and a shower of silk butterflies drifted down from the air. Olivia and Grace cried out and held out their hands to catch one. On the back

of each silk butterfly was a little pin. Grace pinned her butterfly brooch to her T-shirt and Olivia attached hers to her leotard.

"Now you have something to remember us by," Cosmo explained. Grace and Olivia each gave him a kiss on his soft, velvet nose.

"Thank you, Cosmo!" they chorused.

The fairies blew kisses to the girls, and Norris and Hal waved their hats in the air. Even Mossfly stuck his fingers in his mouth and blew a goodbye whistle.

"Farewell!" Miss Rosamund called. "Never forget your special gift!"

The creatures, the classroom and

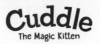

the floating bookcases were already becoming blurred. The girls tingled all over as the magical school faded away ...

***

Olivia opened her eyes. She was curled up inside something small and dark. Grace was squashed next to her, and she could feel Cuddle's whiskers brushing against her arm. She reached up, finding the edge of the container, and pulled herself upright.

"We're inside the dressing-up box in my garden!" Olivia said, climbing out.

Grace swung her legs over the side of the dressing-up box and jumped out too.

"Look! We're still wearing our brooches," Olivia gasped. She stroked the silk butterfly on her leotard and Grace smiled as she peered down at her own brooch.

There was a rustling noise inside the box and Cuddle jumped out, landing on Grace's shoulder. She had a pink feather boa wound around her neck.

"Cuddle's a real glamour-puss," Olivia said, stroking the kitten's silky ears.

Cuddle touched her nose to Olivia's fingers then to Grace's cheek, then hopped to the ground. She ran towards the rose bush and disappeared in a puff of sparkles.

"See you soon, Cuddle!" Olivia called after her.

Grace turned to Olivia. "My tummy's tingling and I feel like floating into the sky," she said. "I think I know what's even more magical than a fairy or an elf!"

Olivia looked puzzled. "What?"

"Being friends!" said Grace, pulling a pirate hat out of the dressing-up box and putting it on her head.

Olivia laughed and put her arm through Grace's. The two girls skipped up the garden path towards the kitchen door. Olivia pushed it open.

"Who needs wands?" she said. "We can make our own magic every day!"

If you enjoyed this book, join Cuddle and best friends Olivia and Grace for three more kitten magic adventures.

In Magical Friends, discover what happens when Cuddle takes Olivia and Grace on an amazing adventure to Ancient Egypt.

ISBN: 978-1-78700-441-2

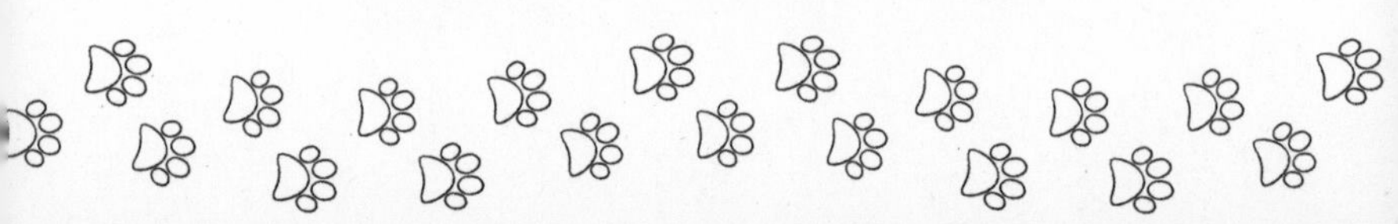

Grace wondered if she was in bed. Maybe she was dreaming about a new friend and a cute kitten. She was lying down, covered in something warm. It didn't feel like her soft duvet, though – it was grainy, and she could move her fingers through it. She opened her eyes and gasped. "Sand!"

The mound of sand next to her stirred and Olivia sat up.

"This is one of your magic tricks, isn't it – like you did with the fence?" Grace asked, feeling silly. "You've made us appear in the sandpit."

But Olivia's eyes were wide with astonishment. "Grace," she said slowly. "We're not in your garden any more."

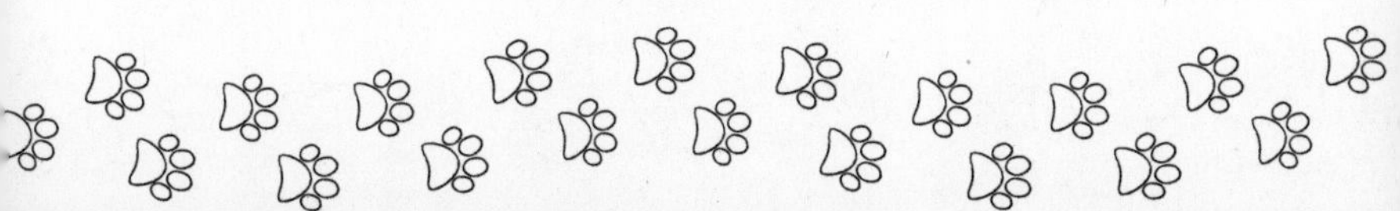

In Superstar Dreams, discover what happens when Cuddle takes Olivia and Grace on an exciting adventure to a top TV talent show.

ISBN: 978-1-78700-447-4

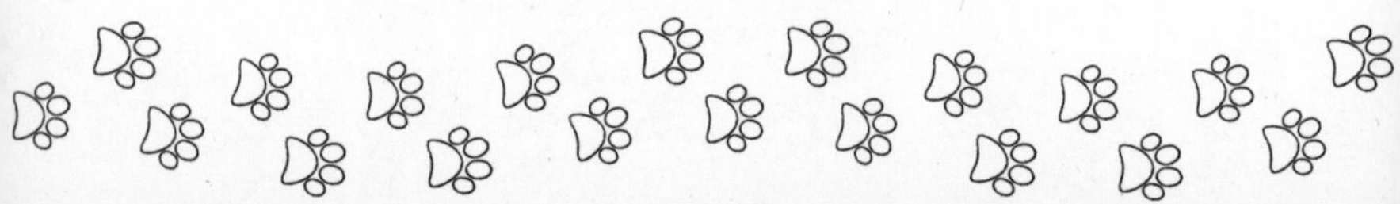

Grace's eyes fluttered open. She was lying on a hard surface in the pitch dark. She closed her eyes and tried opening them again, but it was no good. She couldn't see a thing.

"Olivia?" Grace asked. She could feel her heart thumping.

"I'm here," said Olivia. The two girls were lying side by side.

Olivia knew that Grace was afraid of the dark, and squeezed her friend's hand. "*Where are we?*" she wondered.

Grace rapped the wall above them with her knuckles. It gave a hollow echo.

"That sounds like wood," she said. "I think we're inside some kind of box."

Olivia gulped. "We're trapped!"

In Princess Party Sleepover, join Cuddle as she takes Olivia and Grace on a thrilling royal adventure to a magical masked ball.

ISBN: 978-1-78700-520-4

The girls' eyes fluttered open. Olivia and Grace were still wearing their bedtime clothes and Cuddle had magically given them matching slippers. The evening sky was purple and stars twinkled overhead. A gravel drive stretched before them, edged on either side by flower beds. The drive ended in a bridge, stretching over what looked like a stream.

"It's a moat!" Grace said, pointing at the sparkling water.

On the other side of the bridge was a grand house, its many windows glittering with a golden light.

"It's a palace," Olivia said, clapping her hands.

"So if you see a sunbeam,
and hear Cuddle's bell,
You can join in the
adventure as well!"

Collect the whole set and go on a magical adventure any time you like!